The ROBBER of
FEATHERBED LANE

About The Book

When Ben went next door to tell Sally about his mother's missing diamond ring, they discovered that someone had stolen Sally's banana cake. Then Mrs. Harrington called to them that her pet monkey was gone, and when they went to tell Mary Ann, they found her baby brother had disappeared! A lost kitten was next on the list of thefts, and excitement reached a high pitch, until the last neighbor on Featherbed Lane offered an interesting clue.

The ROBBER of FEATHERBED LANE

by James Holding

illustrated by Laura Jean Allen

Xerox Education Publications

XEROX

For my foster son,
Cheong Kam Fan

The ROBBER of FEATHERBED LANE

Once there was a boy named Benjamin Bostwick Bunker. Everybody called him Ben.

Ben lived in the last house in Featherbed Lane.
Featherbed Lane was a very short street. It had

six houses — four white ones, a yellow one, and
a new one that seemed to be all windows.

One summer afternoon Ben
was throwing a ball against the
side of his house when
his mother called him
from the kitchen window.
"Ben!" she called.
"Please come inside and
help me."
Ben caught his ball
and ran inside.

"I have lost my diamond ring," his mother said.
"I'm sure I put it on the kitchen shelf, but now
it isn't there. Come help me look for it."
They looked and looked, but they could not find it.
"You know what I think?" said Ben. "I think a
robber came into the house and stole it!"
"Now, Ben, you know that isn't so."
"Sally was here this morning," Ben said.
"Yes. Sally borrowed a cup of sugar," his mother
said.
"I'm going to ask her if she has seen the robber!"
said Ben, and ran next door to Sally's house.

Sally was sitting on her swing under the big
willow tree.

"Hi, Sally," called Ben. "Have you seen my
mother's diamond ring?"

"No, Ben," said Sally. "I haven't seen it. Did she
lose it?"

"Yes!" said Ben. "And do you know what I think?
I think a robber came and stole it. Want to help
me catch him?"

Sally laughed. "Oh, Ben! You're always making up
things like that. Last week you said you saw a
tiger in Mr. Miller's yard. Want some banana
cake? Mother made a little one just for me.
It's cooling on the back porch."

They ran around the house
to the porch. "Where's my
banana cake?" cried Sally.
"Mother, did you take my
cake inside?" "No, Sally,
it's cooling on the table there,"
her mother said.
"But, Mother, there's only an
empty plate!" Ben frowned.
"Sally, do you know what I think?
I think there's a robber in Featherbed
Lane. He stole my mother's
diamond ring. And then he stole
your cake!" Someone called from the
yellow house next door. It was
Mrs. Harrington.

"Mr. Link!" she called. "Where are you, Mr. Link?"

"Come on, let's go!" said Ben to Sally.

They ran over to Mrs. Harrington's yard.

"Oh, children, I'm glad to see you," said Mrs. Harrington. "Mr. Link has disappeared. Where could that monkey be?"

They looked everywhere, but Mr. Link was gone.

"Mrs. Harrington," said Ben, "do you know what I think? I think there's a robber in Featherbed Lane. He stole my mother's diamond ring."

"And he stole my banana cake," said Sally.

"And he stole your monkey, too," said Ben. "Let's go ask Mary Ann if she has seen the robber!"

"I'll come with you," said Mrs. Harrington. "Maybe Mary Ann has seen Mr. Link."

All three of them went next door to Mary Ann's house.

"Hi, Mary Ann," called Sally. "What are you looking for under those bushes?"

Mary Ann stood up.

"I'm looking for Douglas," she said. "He was out here eating an ice cream cone a minute ago. Have you seen him?"

Douglas was Mary Ann's two-year-old brother.

"Mary Ann," said Ben, "do you know what we think? We think there's a robber in Featherbed Lane. He stole my mother's diamond ring."

"And he stole my cake," said Sally.

"And he stole my monkey," said Mrs. Harrington.
"But I really don't think he would steal a baby
like Douglas."
"I do! I think the robber stole him!" said Ben.
"So do I," said Sally.
"Let's ask Mr. Miller if he has seen Douglas," cried
Mary Ann.
All four of them ran next door to Mr. Miller's
house.

Mr. Miller lived all alone with his tiger-striped kitten, Pussywillow. He did not like visitors.

"What do you want?" he asked.

"Have you seen my little brother, Douglas?" asked Mary Ann.

"No, I have not seen anyone," said Mr. Miller. "Have *you* seen my tiger-striped kitten, Pussywillow? I've been looking for her everywhere."

"Mr. Miller," said Ben, "do you know what we think? We think there's a robber in Featherbed Lane. He stole my mother's diamond ring."

"And he stole my banana cake," said Sally.

"And my monkey, Mr. Link," said Mrs. Harrington.

"He stole my brother, Douglas, too," said Mary Ann. "Let's go ask Mrs. Merriwether if she has seen the robber!"

All five of them hurried next door. Mrs. Merriwether lived in the new house that seemed
to be all windows. She could see them coming,
so she opened the door.

"How nice of you to call!" said Mrs. Merriwether.

"Have you seen the robber?" asked Ben.

"Robber?" said Mrs. Merriwether. "Is there a robber?"

"He stole my mother's diamond ring," said Ben.

"And my banana cake," said Sally.

"And he stole my monkey, Mr. Link," said Mrs.
Harrington.

"He stole my brother, Douglas, too!" cried Mary
Ann.

"And my kitten, Pussywillow," said Mr. Miller.
Mrs. Merriwether looked as if she knew something.
And she did.

"I haven't seen a robber," she said. "But I *did* see
Pussywillow, just a minute ago, walking across
the street into the park."
"Kitty! Kitty! Kitty!" said Mr. Miller.
All six of them ran across the street into the park.

31

Inside the park they found Pussywillow. She was
eating an ice cream cone in the grass.
Mr. Miller picked up his kitten and hugged her.
"That's Douglas' ice cream cone!" cried Mary Ann.
"He must be here, too!"
They all ran down the path, calling for Douglas.

"Look!" said Mary Ann. "There he is!"
And there was Douglas, laughing and pointing to
the top of a tree.
"Baby!" he was saying. "Baby!"

Mary Ann ran to her little brother.
"Douglas!" she said, picking him up and hugging
him. "You are a naughty boy."

35

"What is Douglas pointing to in that tree?" asked
Ben. "Do you know what I think? I think we've
found the robber! I think he is hiding in the
tree!"
They all looked up into the tree.

Mrs. Harrington laughed.

"That's not the robber," she said. "That's Mr. Link! Come down this very minute, you silly monkey!"

Mr. Link jumped out of the tree into Mrs. Harrington's arms. He was holding something in his paw.

"Look!" cried Sally. "Mr. Link has my banana cake! He has eaten all the banana slices off the top!"

"You give that cake right back to Sally," said Mrs. Harrington to Mr. Link.

Mr. Link handed the cake to Sally.
"I guess we can't eat the cake now," said Sally to
Ben. "Let's give it to the birds."

When she broke the cake into little pieces,
something shiny fell to the ground.
Ben picked it up. "It's my mother's diamond ring!"
he cried. "How did it get into your banana
cake?"
"It must have dropped into the cup of sugar I
borrowed from your mother," said Sally. "And
my mother put the sugar into the cake, diamond
ring and all."
"And Mr. Link took the cake off your back porch
when he smelled the bananas," said Mrs.
Harrington.
"And Douglas followed Mr. Link into the park,"
said Mary Ann, "because he thinks Mr. Link is a
baby, and Douglas loves babies."
"And Pussywillow loves ice cream," said Mr. Miller,
"so *she* followed Douglas to get his ice cream cone."

"So there really was no robber in Featherbed Lane,
after all," said Mrs. Merriwether.

"No," said Ben, "but if there had been one, we
would have caught him for sure!"

"That's right!" everybody said.

Then they all walked back to Featherbed Lane.

KEY WORD LIST

banana

borrowed

brother

cooling

diamond

hiding

hurried

kitchen

kitten

laughing

monkey

naughty

pieces

pointing

robber

shelf

shiny

slices

sugar

summer

tiger-striped

visitors

willow

windows

The Author

JAMES HOLDING, at twelve, sold a piece of verse to a magazine for $3 and became convinced that writing would be his career. After being graduated from Yale, Mr. Holding did the majority of his writing for a leading advertising agency, of which he later became vice-president. Since his retirement, he has authored more than a hundred mystery stories for magazines and television, a dozen juvenile books, teen-age mystery books, and travel articles based on his own worldwide travels.

The Artist

LAURA JEAN ALLEN has illustrated several books for children, as well as adult books, and is well known for her delightful covers for the *New Yorker* magazine. In New York, where she has lived since her graduation from the Pennsylvania Museum School, Miss Allen has done free-lance work in advertising and in fabric and textile design.